# Pray Me A Rainbow

Printed and bound in Canada by Art Bookbindery
www.ArtBookbindery.com

ISBN 978-0-9908803-0-1 (Softcover)
ISBN 978-0-9908803-1-8 (Hardcover)

This book is dedicated to all those who have a
heART of thanksgiving!

For sweet sugar apples
and candy and sleds
For rosy red cheeks
and the hat on my head
For all these things
I thank You.

For orange smiling pumpkins
and soft falling leaves
For crackling fires
and marshmallow treats
For all these things
I thank You.

For bright yellow sunshine
and flowers and bees
For daytime and playtime
and soft summer's breeze
For all these things
I thank You.

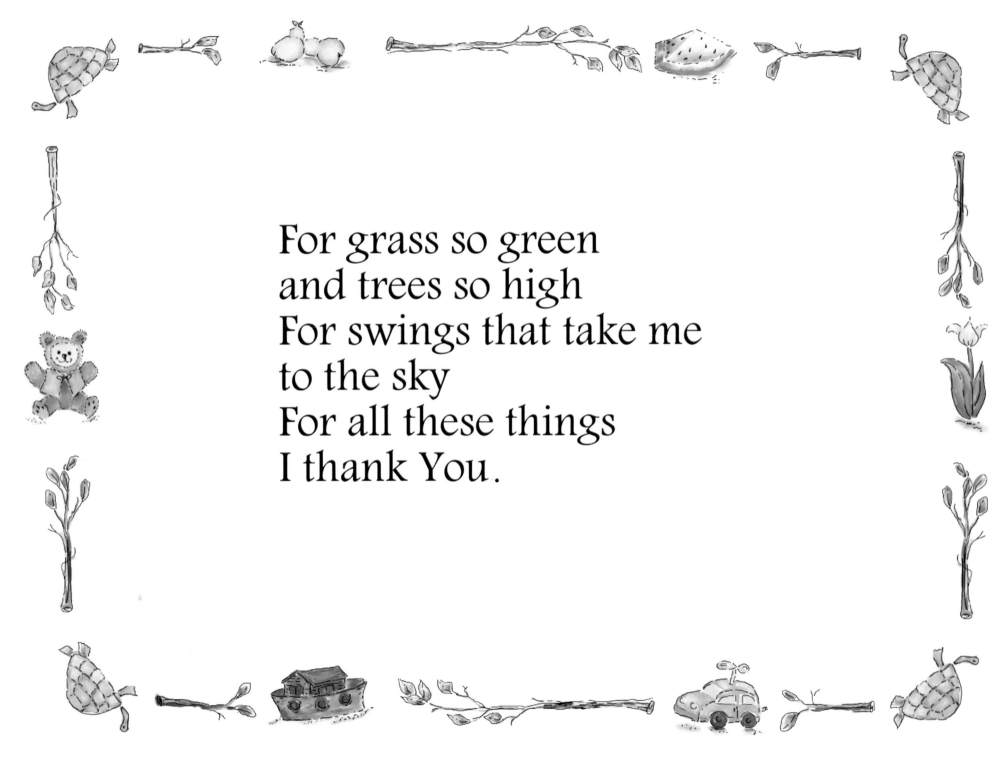

For grass so green
and trees so high
For swings that take me
to the sky
For all these things
I thank You.

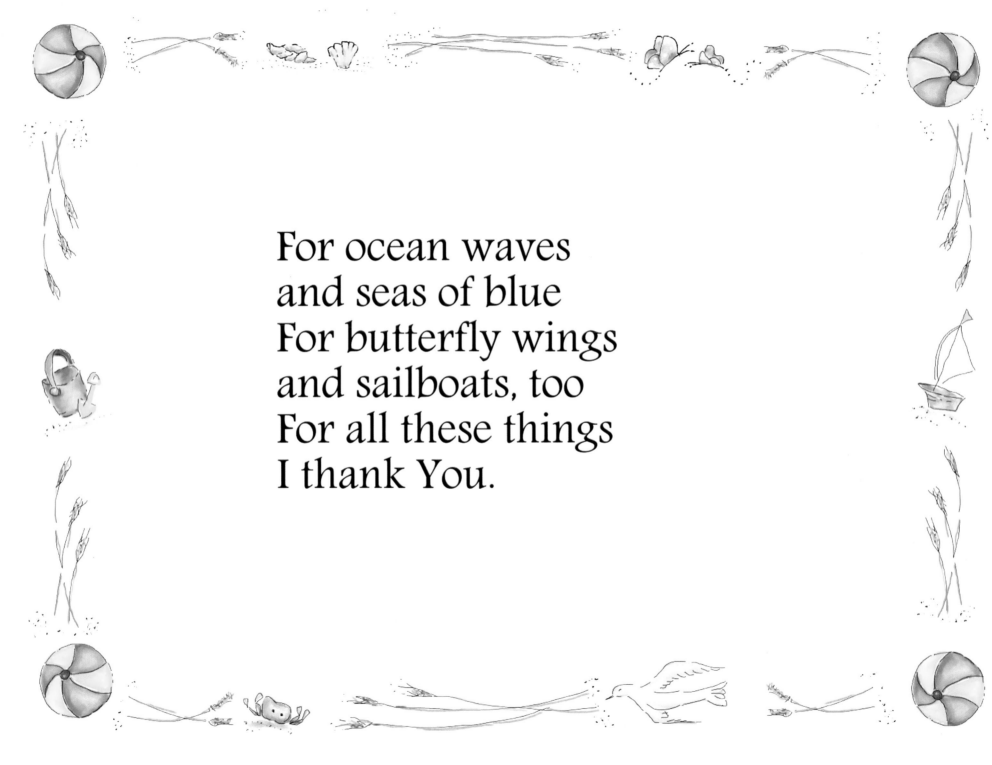

For ocean waves
and seas of blue
For butterfly wings
and sailboats, too
For all these things
I thank You.

For picnics in parks
with kites in the air
For sweet smelling flowers
and bows in my hair
For all these things
I thank You.

Wherever I look,
whatever I see
Your rainbow of blessings
is all around me!

Amen.

# The

# End

# You Can Inspire Thankfulness in Your Child

## Creative ways to Use this Book

 Have your child pick their favorite page in the book. What color is it? What other things can they name that are that color? Pray together and thank God for all the things you can think of that are the same color!

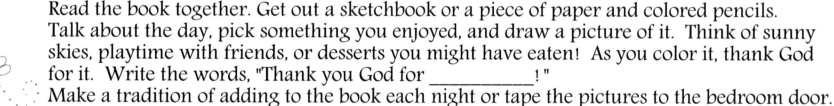 Read the book together. Get out a sketchbook or a piece of paper and colored pencils. Talk about the day, pick something you enjoyed, and draw a picture of it. Think of sunny skies, playtime with friends, or desserts you might have eaten! As you color it, thank God for it. Write the words, "Thank you God for _____!"
Make a tradition of adding to the book each night or tape the pictures to the bedroom door.
Soon, your child will have a beautiful reminder of God's good gifts!
Look at them from time to time and recall the memories!

 Make a prayer chain! As you read through the book, take a colored strip of paper and have your child write down something they are thankful for that is the same color you read about on the page. Staple the strip together to form a chain as you read through the book. Display your paper chain where the child can see it!

"Give thanks to the Lord, for He is good. His love endures forever." Psalm 118